A Kitten in Daisy Street

PAT BELFORD

Illustrated by Martin Cottam

OXFORD

UNIVERSITY PRESS

OXFORD
UNIVERSITY PRESS

Great Clarendon Street, Oxford OX2 6DP

Oxford University Press is a department of the University of Oxford.
It furthers the University's objective of excellence in research, scholarship,
and education by publishing worldwide in

Oxford   New York

Auckland   Cape Town   Dar es Salaam   Hong Kong   Karachi
Kuala Lumpur   Madrid   Melbourne   Mexico City   Nairobi
New Delhi   Shanghai   Taipei   Toronto

With offices in

Argentina   Austria   Brazil   Chile   Czech Republic   France   Greece
Guatemala   Hungary   Italy   Japan   Poland   Portugal   Singapore
South Korea   Switzerland   Thailand   Turkey   Ukraine   Vietnam

Oxford is a registered trade mark of Oxford University Press
in the UK and in certain other countries

British Library Cataloguing in Publication Data
Data available

ISBN-13: 978-0-19-919984-6
ISBN-10: 0-19-919984-1

1 3 5 7 9 10 8 6 4 2

Available in packs
Stage 12 More Stories B Pack of 6:
ISBN-13: 978-0-19-919981-5; ISBN-10: 0-19-919981-7
Stage 12 More Stories B Class Pack:
ISBN-13: 978-0-19-919988-4; ISBN-10: 0-19-919988-4
Guided Reading Cards also available:
ISBN-13: 978-0-19-919990-7; ISBN-10: 0-19-919990-6

Cover artwork by Martin Cottam

Printed in China by Imago

Chapter One

'Hetty! Hetty! The roundabout's coming!'

Emily and Alice ran into the kitchen.

Hetty was washing shirts, up to her elbows in soapy water.

'The roundabout? How do you know?' she asked her little sisters.

'The milk boy told us when we went to pat his horse,' said Alice, excited.

'It's sure to come to a street near us!' added Emily. 'Will you take us to look for it?'

'Me too!' shouted William. He was three years old.

'You can't remember the roundabout.
You were too little last year!' said Alice.

'I can remember! I want to see the
roundabout! Now!' said William.

'Not now,' Hetty told him, 'I
promised Mother that I'd finish this
washing before she gets back.'

'Hurry, Hetty, please!' pleaded the
little girls.

Hetty was only ten. She had been left in charge of her sisters and brothers while their mother was shopping.

There was always a lot of work to do. She rinsed the shirts in a tub of warm water and squeezed them out. Then she went to peg them out to dry. The washing line hung across the street.

Alice and Emily danced round her, getting in the way. 'We want to see the roundabout!' they chanted.

Little William joined in. 'We want to see the roundabout!'

Chapter Two

They all followed Hetty back to the
tiny house.

There was only one room downstairs.
Hetty told her sisters to play outside
while she made the room tidy. She
worked hard.

Later, her brother Tom came in with a bundle of wood for the fire. He was nine and the man of the house, now that their father was dead.

'Mother will need more wood than that to cook the dinner,' Hetty told him, crossly. It was just like Tom to arrive when all the mess had been cleared up. 118

'Billy Carter's seen the roundabout man,' said Tom. 'Will Mother let us go for a ride?'

'I don't know,' said Hetty, 'but she has no money to spare. It was a penny a ride last year and there are five of us.'

Mother arrived back from shopping. She carried a basket full of potatoes and carrots.

'Mother, the roundabout man's coming!'

'I've no money for roundabouts. There's only enough left to pay the rent.'

Tom and Hetty looked at each other, disappointed. They loved the roundabout with its painted horses and tinkling music.

'Go and fetch some water. And take the little ones with you. I want to clean the bedroom. Alice! Emily! William!'

Carrying buckets and jugs, the five
children hurried along the cobbled
street to the old black pump. Everyone
in the street got their water from the
pump.

The children took turns to work the pump handle.

The water splashed into the buckets and on to the bare feet of the three little ones. Only Hetty and Tom wore boots. Mother was saving to buy boots for the others, before winter came.

At last the job was done. They walked home, carefully, with the heavy buckets. They tried not to spill any. If they spilt some they would have to go back for more. There was no tap in the house.

A family of six used a lot of water in a day.

When the water had been carried home safely, Mother said, 'Now, Hetty, you can take Mrs Dyson's clean washing back to Cherry Tree House.' Mother took in washing to earn extra money.

Doing the washing and carrying water had made Hetty very tired, but she had to do as Mother said. She picked up Mrs Dyson's big bundle of clean washing. She took the empty purse for the money and set off.

Chapter Three

It was a long, long walk. Cherry Tree
House stood at the far end of Daisy
Street.

As Hetty got nearer, she heard
music – *plinkety plonk, plinkety plonk.*
She knew that tune.

The roundabout! she thought.
When she turned the corner into
Daisy Street, there it was!

The roundabout was set on a cart. An old brown horse pulled it from street to street so that the children could have rides. Hetty saw the old horse had his nosebag on and was eating his dinner.

The roundabout had stopped going round and children were climbing on to the painted, wooden horses.

The roundabout man took their money and turned the handle.

The music played again – *plinkety plonk, plinkety plonk*.

The painted horses went round and round, slowly at first and then faster.

Hetty went up to the man. 'Please, mister, how much is it?'

'A penny a ride, same as last year.'

Hetty sighed. It would cost five pence for them all. Mother would never be able to spare five pence.

'Do you want a ride?' asked the roundabout man, kindly.

Hetty shook her head, sadly.

'Later, maybe?' he asked. 'I'll be here all day!'

She smiled, then stood and watched other children having rides. Some lucky ones went on twice.

They were all laughing as they whirled round. Riding on the roundabout was exciting.

Soon, Hetty remembered the washing she was carrying. She hurried along to Mrs Dyson's house.

CHERRY TREE HOUSE

She walked through the wide gateposts and along a path to the back door of Cherry Tree House.

In the big garden, Mrs Dyson's two little boys were playing with hobby-horses.

Hetty could see that they wore smart clothes and shiny brown leather boots and woollen stockings. They were about the same ages as Alice and Emily.

She wondered what it must be like to be rich and live in such a big house.

Cherry Tree House had rows and rows of windows and six chimney pots. Six! She knocked on the back door.

Mrs Dyson's cook answered it.

'Oh, you've brought the washing! Come in, love!' she said. She listened for a moment. 'What's that music?'

'It's the roundabout,' replied Hetty. 'It's come to Daisy Street.'

She stood in the big kitchen while the cook fetched some money to pay for the washing. When the cook gave Hetty the coins, she put them carefully away in her purse.

The cook gave her a big warm, sticky bun. She always had a bun for Hetty.

'Eat that, love,' she said. 'I expect you'll be having a ride on the roundabout?'

'I … er, I don't think so. There are five of us. Mother can't afford it. It's a lot of money.'

Hetty sat on a big chair to eat her bun. It was delicious.

When she had finished, she licked her fingers and thanked the cook, and got down from the chair.

'Bless you. Tell your mother that I'll send some more washing on Friday,' said the kind cook.

She dropped something into Hetty's apron pocket.

'There are a few pennies so that you can all go on the roundabout.'

'Oh, thank you!' gasped Hetty and she ran outside and along the path to Daisy Street.

Chapter Four

Outside the gates of Cherry Tree House, she stopped to count the pennies. There were five. *Five!* And all with the head of the queen, Victoria, on them. *Wait till I tell the others*, thought Hetty.

An old wooden box stood on the pavement.

As Hetty put the coins in her pocket, she thought she saw something move. Something in the box. Something grey and furry.

She peeped into the box.

'A kitten!' she whispered, and gazed at the fluffy grey animal. She picked it up. It was very tiny. She could feel its soft bones. The kitten opened its mouth and Hetty saw the little pink tongue.

'Oh, you are so pretty!'

She looked round. An old woman was passing by.

'Has anyone lost a kitten?' asked Hetty.

'Not that I know of. It's been there
in that box since this morning.
Nobody wants it. It has been left to
die, I should think!'

'Oh, no! It mustn't die!' cried Hetty.

'Then you look after it,' said the old
woman, 'because no one else will!'

She walked away.

Hetty stroked the kitten's soft fur.
She could not leave the kitten to die.

'I'll call you Flossie,' she whispered.

Carrying Flossie carefully, she went
back along Daisy Street to the
roundabout.

She went up to the roundabout man.

'Has anyone lost a kitten?' she asked.

'A kitten? Nobody's said anything to me about a kitten.'

The roundabout man scratched his head.

'You keep it. Take it home.'

Hetty walked on. In May Street she passed the baker's shop. Old Mr Brown was sweeping the path outside the doorway.

'Have you come to buy some bread?' he asked.

Hetty shook her head. 'I found this kitten in Daisy Street. Has anyone lost it?' she asked.

'Nobody that I've heard about,' said Mr Brown. 'It's a grand little animal. You take it home and give it some milk.'

Hetty walked on. She had to keep the kitten.

'You're so pretty, Flossie,' she whispered, and stroked the soft grey fur.

She was almost home. What would Mother say? There would be trouble, Hetty was sure.

Back home, the house was very noisy. William was crying. He had fallen and cut his knee. Mother was washing the knee and putting on a bandage. Alice and Emily were fighting over an old doll. Tom was shouting at them.

Hetty knew that this was not a good time to show Mother the kitten. Quickly, she hid Flossie in her apron pocket and ran upstairs to the bedroom.

She took some clothes out of her drawer and popped Flossie in. She closed the drawer, all but a small gap, so the kitten could breathe.

'I'll bring you some milk later, Flossie,' she whispered, 'promise!' Then she ran downstairs.

The kitchen was quieter now. Emily and Alice had stopped fighting and William had stopped crying. Mother was stirring the stew. Tom was outside, chopping wood.

Soon it was time for dinner. The family sat round the bare wooden table. Mother served vegetable soup with some bread. There was no meat because it was too expensive.

They sat quietly with their food. The children were not allowed to speak while they were eating, unless Mother asked them something.

'We may be poor, but good manners cost nothing,' Mother often said.

All through dinner, Hetty thought about the kitten.

Somehow she would have to give Flossie some milk. But how? She and Tom only had water to drink. The milk had to be saved for the little ones.

William, who was still upset after his fall, didn't want to drink his milk.

Hetty watched carefully, as sometimes her little brother spilled his milk on purpose.

When the meal was over, Hetty and Tom had to clear away and wash up.

Mother went outside to fetch the dry washing.

Hetty grabbed William's cup and a clean saucer and ran upstairs with the milk.

When she opened the drawer, the kitten mewed sadly.

'Here's your dinner, Flossie.' Hetty poured the milk into the saucer. She stroked the soft fur for a moment, then she part-closed the drawer again.

'Hurry up, Hetty! I'm doing all the work!' called Tom.

She hurried downstairs. She longed to tell Tom about the kitten, but Emily and Alice were playing in the kitchen. They couldn't keep secrets.

She dried the dishes and put them on the shelf.

'Hetty! Come out here and help me fold these sheets!' called Mother.

She sounded cross. Hetty decided to say nothing about Flossie until the next day. She must keep her secret.

Chapter Five

She looked in the milk jug. There was not much milk left. The kitten would need another drink before bedtime.

Hetty helped Mother with the sheets.

Emily and Alice danced in the kitchen. They got very silly.

Alice fell and sat in a bucket of washing. *Splash!* Alice screamed. Water was everywhere. Her clothes were wet.

Mother was angry. She took off Alice's dress, petticoat and drawers, and found some dry clothes.

Then she sent Alice and Emily upstairs to play in the bedroom. 'Be good girls and don't quarrel!' she said.

Hetty mopped up the water and hung the wet clothes outside.

Suddenly, there was a shout. Emily and Alice ran downstairs.

'Mother, Mother! We've found a kitten!'

'She was in Hetty's drawer!' added Alice.

Hetty gasped.

'What?' asked Mother.

'Look!' Emily held Flossie. Alice stroked her.

'Do you know anything about this, Hetty?' asked Mother, in her angry voice.

'I found it in Daisy Street, when I went to Mrs Dyson's with the washing. Nobody wants it. I couldn't leave it to die!' There were tears in Hetty's eyes.

'We can't keep a kitten,' Mother said. 'We've hardly enough money to feed ourselves. Kittens need milk!'

'I'll earn some money. I'll run errands for people!' said Hetty. 'I'll do anything to have it for my own!'

'Oh, please, please, let us keep it!' begged Alice.

'It's beautiful!' said Emily.

William wanted to hold the kitten. 'What's it called?' he asked.

'Flossie,' whispered Hetty.

'I'm very angry with you, Hetty,' said Mother. 'It was wrong of you to hide an animal in the bedroom!'

'Please, Mother, don't send it away!' said Tom. 'It could catch mice when it's a bit older.'

'*Meow!*'

'Flossie's hungry!' said Emily.

Mother did a surprising thing. She poured some milk into a bowl and held the kitten on her lap to drink.

They all watched as the little pink tongue flicked in and out. Soon the milk was gone. Mother stroked Flossie's fur.

'Please may we keep her?' begged Hetty.

Tom interrupted. 'Never mind about the kitten. I want to have a ride on the roundabout!'

'So do I!' said William.

'Hurrah! Roundabout!' shouted Alice and Emily.

'Be quiet!' scolded Mother. 'I told you that I've no money to spare!'

Suddenly, Hetty remembered the five pennies in her apron pocket.

'Mrs Dyson's cook gave me five pennies. It's for us all to go on the roundabout.'

'I hope you didn't beg for money!' said Mother, sharply.

'No, we were talking about the roundabout. She just gave it to me.'

Hetty laid the five pennies on the table.

'One each.' She gave the fifth penny to Mother. 'That's to buy milk for Flossie. If you let us keep her, I don't want a ride on the roundabout.'

Mother was still stroking the kitten.

'I'll have to think about it,' she said. 'You should have asked me first, before you brought the kitten into the house.'

Tom picked up the four pennies. 'Come on, let's go on the roundabout!'

He dashed out of the door. The other children followed.

Hetty stopped by the door and looked back. Mother had Flossie and she was smiling.

She handed Flossie to Hetty. 'Show Flossie the roundabout!'

'Come on!' William tugged her hand.

Hetty walked along the streets, holding the kitten.

The four younger ones ran ahead to Daisy Street. Would they be too late?

'It's still there!' yelled Tom, as they turned the corner.

He gave three of the pennies to the roundabout man, then Hetty appeared and he turned to her.

'You can have my penny to buy milk for the kitten too,' he told her, shyly. 'I don't mind missing a ride.'

'Oh, Tom, thank you!'

Tom smiled. He helped Alice and Emily climb on to the horses.

Hetty lifted William on to a white horse with a black mane and a gold-painted harness. 'Hold tight,' she whispered as the music began to play – *plinkety plonk, plinkety plonk.*

Then Alice, Emily and William rode their roundabout horses. Slowly at first, then faster and faster they whirled round and round.

Tom and Hetty watched and Hetty stroked Flossie, their new kitten.

About the author

I was a primary school
teacher for many years
and I encouraged all
my pupils to write
stories. I've always
been fascinated by
the Victorians and
was inspired to write

this book after seeing the old horse-
drawn roundabout in a folk museum.

I've written eight other children's
books and several musical plays, two of
which have a Victorian theme. One of
the plays was adapted for television.

I live in Yorkshire with my husband
and I like walking in the Dales.